BEST MEME FROM WEB 2023-2024

This is a book that wants to testify as the irony and conception
general joke has been modified at the time of Internet,
Understood as a genuine generational change.

In order to collect information, please express your opinion on the following link.

THIS IS THE UGLIEST BOOK EVER!
BUT IT WILL BE THE ONE THAT YOU GIVE MORE
SATISFACTION!
YOU'LL FIND SOME APHORISMS INSIDE
WORTHY OF THE...

LAUGHTER IS GOOD!
WE HOPE IT HELPS YOU TO UNPLUG
AND GET HIGH!

HAVE FUN!!!

REMEMBER
TO MAKE THE REVIEW A 5-STAR
ON AMAZON!!!
DON'T BE LAZY...
I MADE THIS BOOK
TO MAKE YOU HAPPY...

THE MINIMUM IS TO RETURN THE COURTESY!

CIA'!

"I'll grant you 7 wishes!
"Wasn't it just three?"
"Yes, but you're a bit in
the shit!"

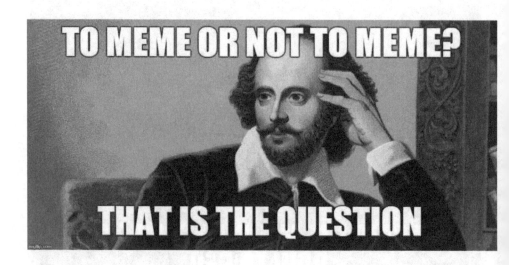

"-I love big boobs!"
"-Mr Newton we can't say this!!!"
-"ok ...write: larger the mass, greater the force of attraction!"

Whoever left this by the dumpster, please take it back immediately! Tonight it's gonna rain and we've got enough problems

SOMETIMES I READ MEMES

AND I HAVE NO IDEA WHAT THEY MEAN.

When Christmas shopping didn't bankrupt you

What if I told you

Not all cats hate water.

when you behaved badly in public

And your mother could not reproach you

Prepping for a week-long vacation, but your boss assigns you last-minute projects.

...and those who take the photo with the tower of Pisa... silence!

Vegetables in the fridge
watching you order takeaway

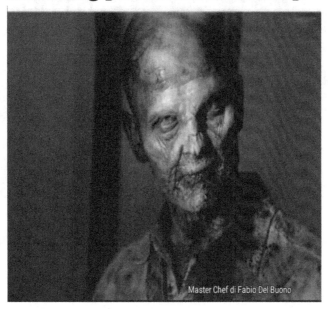

Master Chef di Fabio Del Buono

Running out of eggnog with 20 guests at the door

By drinking 130 bottles of wine
we can save a bird!

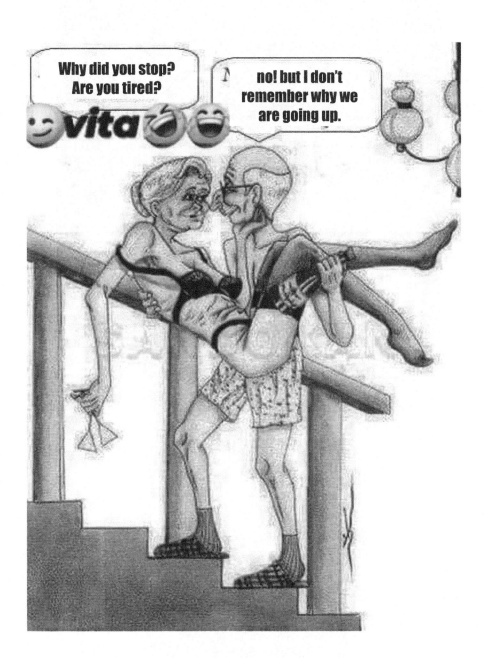

Call your dog "shark" and take it to the sea, maybe not a good idea!

What you seek is already within you!

At the supermarket:
-Excuse me, are you guys lining up?
- No we met here to make the train...
soon we leave!

I don't know if to cook it or ask it if there is something wrong.

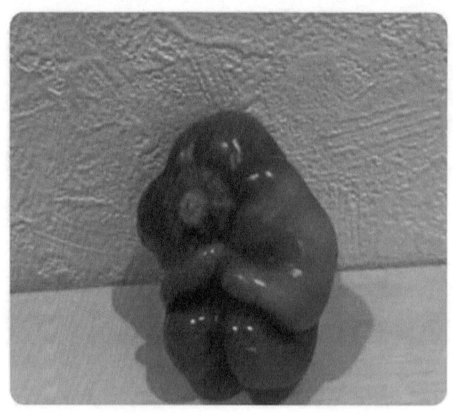

Mom told me not to touch it

Me while I think about whether
to start working
or living off my beauty!

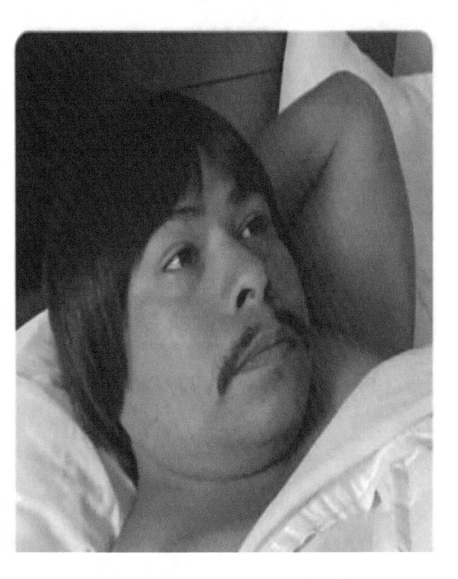

https://www.facebook.com/manuela.cardello/

I who happily go to meet another shitty day!

https://www.facebook.com/manuela.cardello/

https://www.facebook.com/manuela.cardello/

beach in china

If you lose your son, don't look for him,
Make another one!

when you are in a hurry to pay an urgent bill... the post office employee!

I need advice...
What could I do with this space?

tradotto

Do you have a magical nephew that you hate?

Don't know if I should say hello,
ask for an autograph
or report it to the museum!

https://www.facebook.com/manuela.cardello/

I DO SOMETHING ELSE, INSTEAD OF DOING SOMETHING I REALLY HAVE TO DO!

IT'S HARD TO FIND THE RIGHT BRIDE... BUT THE PHOTOGRAPHER IS ALSO IMPORTANT!

THE DOG IS THE BEST THERAPY FOR YOUR PROBLEMS.
MY DOG AFTER SHARING ALL MY PROBLEMS

WHEN YOU SEE YOUR WIFE
IN THE AUDIENCE YELLING
"HORNY REFEREE"

Black Friday sales

Holiday peer pressure

Guilt-tripping ads

Overspending on Christmas gifts

THE DRAINING RED BERRY TEA THAT LOOKS AT YOU AFTER CHRISTMAS LUNCH

https://besti.it/9

You're awesome! Honey, the way you remembered to put the toilet seat down deserves a standing ovation!

When you think you're in charge, but your wife reminds you who the real boss is

When your wife asks you to explain why you bought another gaming console

Man with a PhD who fixes the simplest issue alone

Locking away my chips to avoid temptation

IT DOESN'T MATTER WHERE YOU HIDE YOUR HUSBAND

I'll look HIM.... I'll FIND HIM I'll FUCK HIM

I DON'T CARE ABOUT THE BEER BRAND... BUT THE CHAIR!

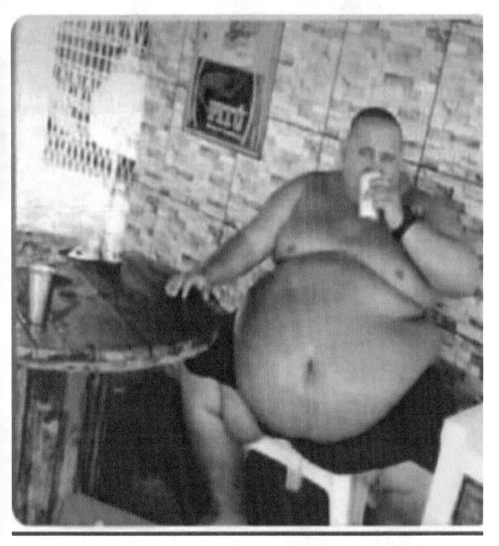

INSIDE YOU THERE ARE TWO WOLVES

Your desire for that delicious cheesecake

Your plan to start eating healthy

AND TODAY WE WOKE UP BEAUTIFUL, FRESH, HAPPY AND CAREFREE

I SAW A MAN DIE FOR LOVE

https://www.facciabuco.com/post/1600477aqq/vaccata-erotica-post-by-garak.html

"MOM, SCHOOL HASN'T STARTED!"
"I know but you start walking slowly."

https://www.facebook.com/Leesaurite/?locale=te_IN

Me adding a new hairstyle to my look!

When you find out your favorite movie was removed from Netflix

When your stomach starts making weird noises during a meeting

Fitness goals

Me

Junk food cravings

THE REASON WHY JAPANESE PEOPLE RESPECT THEIR MOTHERS

WHEN I TRY TO BE SOCIAL AND POSITIVE

I just passed the phone!
THE OTHER GIRLS

ME!

I ASK FOR A FRIEND...
BUT IS SILVESTER STALLION?

THAT'S WHY ELSA IS A QUEEN AND THE OTHERS ONLY PRINCESSES!

Thursday

299€

Friday

299€

Black Friday

~~499€~~

299€

wait

wait

NOW!!!

I WHO, AFTER EATING THE TABLES, TRUST IN THE FENNEL HERBAL TEA TO LOSE WEIGHT

WHEN SUDDENLY THE TEMPERATURES DROP BUT YOU DON'T WANT TO GIVE UP ELEGANCE

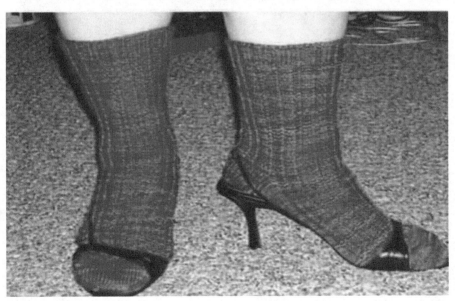

https://www.facebook.com/manuela.cardello/

When you come home and realize the dog chewed your favorite shoes again

Me on my way to procrastinate instead of working

FEEL THE MAGIC OF CHRISTMAS COMING?
ME...

WHEN YOU RELAX IN THE EVENING AFTER INTERACTING WITH THE WORLD

When it's Monday and your alarm clock rings.

I WILL NOT ORDER MORE SHIT ON WISH

ME

THE LADLE OF LOCH NESS

I open the window so there's a little air

When it's Monday morning and your to-do list is glaring at you

Coworker who always volunteers for extra tasks but doesn't actually do them

My job here is done

The employee who ends up doing all the

But you didn't do anything

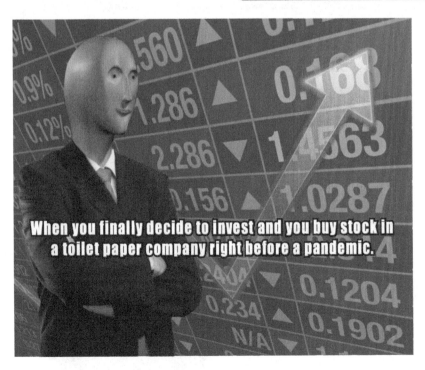

When you finally decide to invest and you buy stock in a toilet paper company right before a pandemic.

https://www.facebook.com/dsambienti.it/?locale=en_GB

https://www.gqitalia.it/lifestyle/article/sneakers-lidl-meme

a person realistically pondering their next struggle

And now we see if you retire.
Follow me for more tips...

Divinity sighted in Italic coast

NINE MONTHS IN MY WOMB...
12 HOURS OF LABOR...
100 NIGHTS WITHOUT SLEEP...
AND IT'S ALL HIS FATHER

When your expectations meet reality

WHAT A SWEET LITTLE ANGEL... I CAN'T WAIT TO FUCK HIM UP!

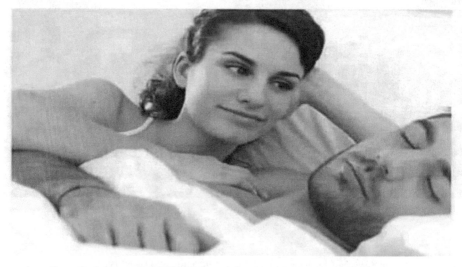

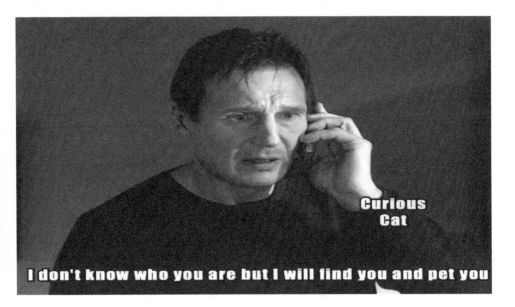

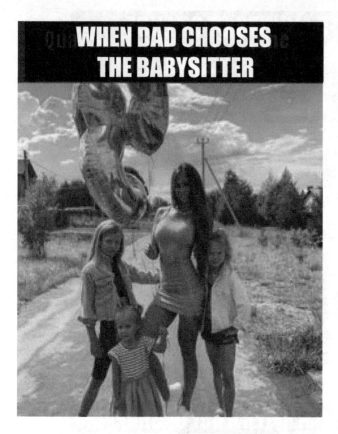

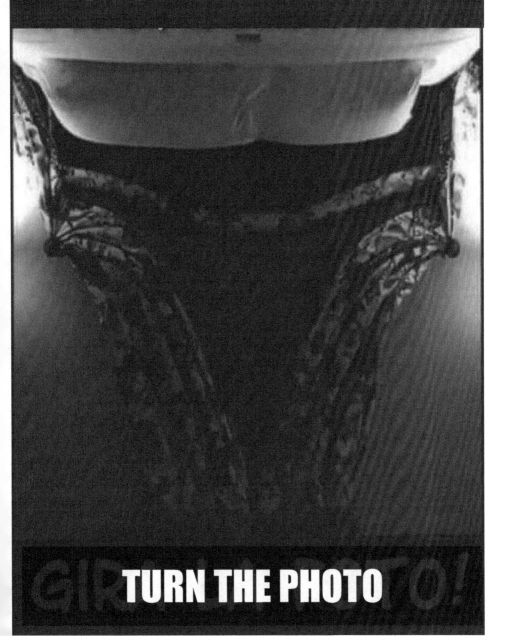

watch from afar

MY DAD CRIED FOR A WHOLE DAY FROM EMOTION

WHEN YOU ARRIVE IN THAT AGE WHERE YOU ARE NOT WATCHING THE MOVIE, BUT IT IS THE MOVIE THAT WATCHES YOU!

When you get jealous of your friend's success
So you have chosen... death.

Girlfriend wants a romantic vacation 😆
Shut up and take my money!

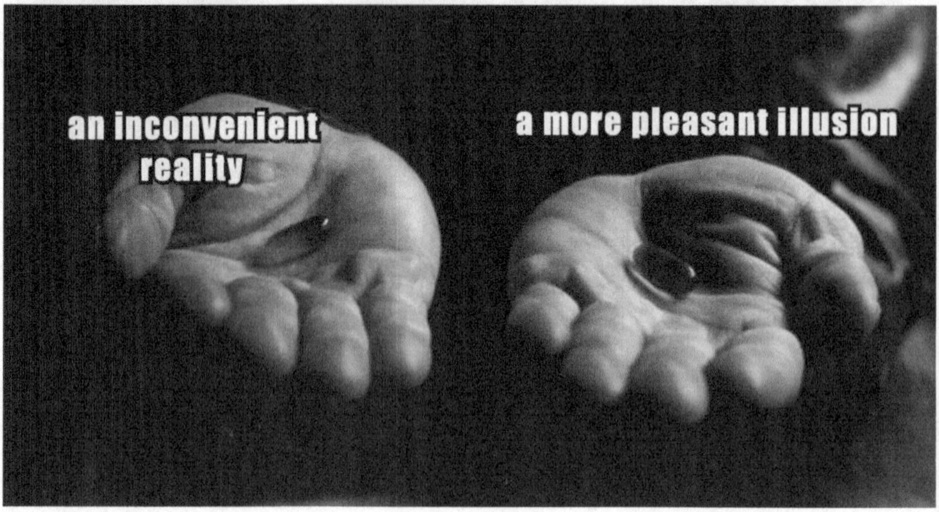
an inconvenient reality
a more pleasant illusion

When you see your ex moving on

When you get a promotion at the same company before them

when you poop at someone else's house and the toilet doesn't flush

Why are you always late to pick me up from school, Dad?

Traffic.

By the way, I bought a new video game console, wanna guess which one?

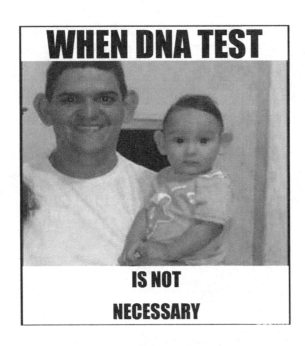

https://www.corriere.it/tecnologia/meme/cards/giornata-gatto-meme-piu-divertenti-festeggiare-nostri-amici-felini/gatto-inquisitore.shtml

https://it.memedroid.com/memes/detail/690312

Accidentally knocking over the Christmas tree

Shopping for Christmas

THIS WAS THE PRINCESS OF PERSIA. SHE HAD MORE THAN 100 SUITORS, AND 13 OF THEM TOOK THEIR OWN LIVES WHEN SHE REFUSED. YOU'RE NOT UGLY, YOU JUST HAVE THE WRONG TIME!

Gonna surprise everyone by buying their favorite snacks.

Forgetting mom put all of them on a diet.

https://www.facebook.com/Sorridomentreaffogo/

https://www.facebook.com/catnkittenclub/photos/a.186550158643415/969610760337347/?paipv=0&eav=AfZwB-9D4xqq7xxPBqd8OUpbOiIY7T0_lOShJtm6V1VDwhzkv-L9y2OzLPaQJxCybMUU&_rdr

INVISIBLE BIKE

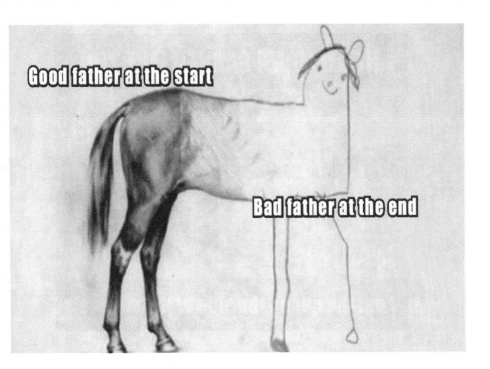

Good father at the start

Bad father at the end

Dad during math problems

When you open your kid's homework for the first time and realize you've forgotten everything

HELLO LOVE I PARKED LIKE YOU

I put the car on the side of the sidewalk

https://besti.it/51429/Pronto-amoree-Ho-parcheggiato-come-hai-detto-tu-Ho-messo

https://twitter.com/LucaCico80/status/1063497245952274433

When you teach your grandmother how to use emojis and she thinks 'LOL' means 'Lots of Love'

Getting all dressed up for work at 7 AM

Realizing it's a holiday and going back to bed

https://besti.it/51429/Pronto-amoree-Ho-parcheggiato-come-hai-detto-tu-Ho-messo

GOODBYE TO THE NEXT VOLUME!

WE CLOSE WITH THE MUSIC VIDEO MOST BEAUTIFUL EVER!

Made in the USA
Monee, IL
13 November 2024

69960103R10056